Ski Paw-trol

A Vanessa Abbot Cat Cozy Mystery Series

Book Seven

Nancy C. Davis

C O N T E N T S

❖

CHAPTER 1

————— ❖ —————

Pete Wheeler gripped the steering wheel with white knuckles and squinted through the front windshield. The headlight beams ended in a vast blackness a few feet in front of the car. Then from the darkness, white flurries would swirl around the car. The wiper blades packed snow into a tight ring around the windshield.

Vanessa glanced at Pete's pinched face and cleared her throat. "Thanks again for letting me bring the cats to the ski lodge. I hope they won't be too much bother."

Pete compressed his lips, but he didn't take his eyes off the road. He leaned forward to peer out into the dark. "I'm sure it will be fine. Flossy,

Henry, and Aurora are well-behaved cats.

Vanessa glanced over the seat back. The three cats lay curled in their carrier box on the back seat, sound asleep. "I'm sure they'll be fine, too. I don't think I could leave them behind."

"I know you couldn't," he replied, "and I want you to be comfortable. This is your first vacation away from the Sanctuary. I'm glad Sam Powell could take over for you while you're away. You need a weekend off."

"Sam will do a wonderful job," Vanessa agreed. "He's proven himself such an asset since he started working with us."

"He'll be a full vet in his own right soon," Pete went on. "Then what will you do without him?"

"He said he plans to settle in the area," Vanessa

told him. "And now that Maggie is spending more time tending race horses, she's ready to give up her dog and cat practice to someone else. This could be the perfect opportunity for both of them."

Pete nodded. "Then you'll have to find someone else to take over for you when you go on vacation."

Vanessa cast another look into the back seat. The cats hadn't moved. "I hope there's enough room for them to move around. You know how they like to go exploring."

"The photos I saw online of the Dove's Peak Ski Lodge show plenty of space," Pete went on. "The rooms are big, and my friend Robert who got us the Bargain Booking said the service is excellent. He ought to know. He's the manager."

"I hope he doesn't consider your request an

imposition," Vanessa murmured.

"Why would he?" Pete asked. "He's my oldest friend. We went to college together."

"You said you haven't seen him in five years," Vanessa pointed out.

"We're still friends," Pete told her. "Friendship doesn't end just because you haven't seen each other in a while."

"I'm just saying I hope he doesn't consider this an imposition," Vanessa replied.

"You don't have to worry about that," Pete told her. "Oh, look. Here's the turn off at last."

The headlights reflected off a bright green sign looming in the dark. *Dove's Peak Ski Lodge, 1/2 mile. Welcome.* Pete sighed with relief, and the car struggled through the last treacherous stretch of the storm. Blazing lights cut the night and lit up the snow surrounding a big timber frame building. Snow mounded on top of the cars in the parking lot.

Pete parked by the front door, and three young men wrapped up to their eyeballs in hats, scarves, and mittens ran out of the building. The first held out his hand for the car keys. "You go right on in, Sir. I'll park your car for you, and Jimmy here will bring your luggage."

Pete handed over the keys, and Jimmy heaved the suitcases out of the trunk. Vanessa lifted the cat carriers out of the back seat. "Don't worry about that, Ma'am. Tim will get that for you."

Vanessa held onto the carrier. "That's all right. I'd rather carry it myself."

Tim backed off, and the three men hurried about their work. Pete grabbed the other two carriers with Henry and Flossy. He turned to watch the car drive off and disappear into the snowdrifts. "Now that's what I call service."

"On a night like this, it's the least they can do," Vanessa replied. "We'd be out here for hours just trying to get through the front door."

Tim waved toward the entrance. "If you folks follow me, we'll get you checked in right away."

A blast of warm air hit them when they entered the lobby, and Vanessa shook the snowflakes out of her hair. A fire blazed in a big stone fireplace surrounded by leather couches. The spicy aroma of pine needles and cinnamon filled the lodge.

Pete and Vanessa followed Tim to the front desk,

and the clerk handed them their key. "Your room is right down that hall there. Make yourselves at home, and the Concierge will be down in a minute to make sure you have everything you need."

"Thank you." Vanessa picked up the cat carrier, and she and Pete followed the hall to the far end. The hall ended at a locked fire escape. "That's weird. I don't see any room numbers."

Pete frowned. "Maybe the clerk made a mistake."

They retraced their steps back along the hall and inspected every sign on every door. "Here's the linen closet, and this one says *Staff*. There isn't a guest room anywhere along this hall."

"Let's go back to the front desk," Pete suggested. "The clerk can tell us where to find the room."

The clerk smiled when they approached the desk. "No, that's right. Your room is in the Staff Section."

Vanessa's jaw dropped. "The Staff Section? But we're paying guests. There must be some mistake."

The clerk squinted at his computer. "There's no mistake. It says right here you used the Bargain Booking, and that's the room you booked."

Pete shook his head and turned away. "If they're selling the room to guests, it can't be too bad. Come on."

They continued along the hallway. Vanessa shifted the cat carrier to her other hand to give her aching fingers a rest. By the time they got back to the room with the *Staff* sign on the door, she couldn't hold it up any longer. She set it down and stretched her back.

Pete took a deep breath and unlocked the door. "How bad can it be?"

The door swung back, and they froze in their tracks. Neither crossed the threshold. A single tiny window sat high up the far wall, and a bare light bulb hung from the ceiling. A set of bunk beds stood on one side of the small room with just enough space to walk between them and the wall.

Pete swept the room with his eyes. Vanessa dared not say a word. Neither of them set foot in that room. Henry peered out from his carrier and meowed.

At that moment, a brisk young woman with tussled strawberry-blonde hair strode down the hall. She beamed at Pete and Vanessa. "So you found your room all right? I'm Sally Bendall. I'm Concierge of the Dove's Peak Ski Lodge. If there's anything I can get you to make your stay more comfortable, be sure to let me know."

"There is," Pete snapped. "You can get us a bigger room."

Sally's eyes flew open. "But this is the Bargain Booking room. This is the room you booked."

"My friend Robert Ipswich is the manager of this lodge," Pete replied. "He booked this room for us because it was affordable. He never said anything about it being a staff room or a closet with bunk beds. We're not staying here. We paid a lot of money to spend our vacation at this lodge, and you're going to give us a real room with a real bed—no ifs, ands, or buts."

"It was Robert who sent me to find out if you were happy with your room," Sally told him. "He invited you to our *End of Season* Party in the dining hall."

Pete scowled at the room. "I've known Robert Ipswich since high school. He always was a prankster. I hope this isn't his idea of a twisted joke."

"The room comes with all the benefits of the lodge," Sally told him. "It comes with all you can eat in the dining hall and full access to the bar and spa at no extra charge. The room really is a bargain."

Vanessa spoke up. "I'm sure it will be fine. We both need a massage after the trip we just had up the mountain in that snow storm."

Sally burst into a radiant smile. "I'll make the appointment for you right away."

Vanessa watched her bustle down the hall. "She seems nice."

Pete rubbed his chin. "I guess so—but the staff room?"

She patted his arm. "This is fine for us. You saw the booking prices of the other rooms, and we could never afford them. Let's stay here and be happy with it. We don't have to come back here except to sleep, and no one will complain about us keeping three cats in this room."

She popped the latches on the cat carriers. At first, nothing moved inside the carriers. Then Henry poked his nose out and took a ginger step into the room. He sniffed the air and twitched his whiskers in the direction of the lower bunk bed.

Flossy strode out of her carrier after him and pretended not to look right or left. She marched straight into the middle of the room and sat down to lick her chest. Then she sneezed. Aurora frisked into the room and jumped onto the top bunk. In an instant, she burrowed under the blankets and disappeared. Flossy blinked up at her. Then she hopped up onto the lower bunk and stretched herself out along the pillow. Henry narrowed his eyes at Vanessa.

Vanessa sat down on the bottom bunk, and Henry jumped into her lap. Vanessa ran her hand down his back. "This is perfect. The cats are comfortable, so the room can't be all bad."

Pete frowned. "I'm glad the cats are happy. The question is, where am I going to sleep?"

CHAPTER 2

— ❖ —

A tumult of voices and clinking crystal echoed out of the dining room as Pete and Vanessa approached the party. A band played rousing twenties swing music, and Vanessa couldn't stop her foot tapping. Black-tied carried trays of champagne flutes around the room and offered them to anyone who cared to take one. Tables laden with food lined the room, and men and women in evening dress filled the dining hall.

Pete and Vanessa paused at the door. "Is this supposed to be a staff party?"

Pete shifted from one foot to the other. "I didn't know it was black tie. I've never been so underdressed in my life."

A man with salt-and-pepper grey hair strode toward them. He stuck out his hand to Pete. "There you are, Wheeler. Always late. I've been waiting hours for you to show up. Where have you been?"

"I got lost in a broom closet behind the boiler room," Pete grumbled. "I had to wait for the janitor to unlock the door and let me out."

The man's eyes popped open. Then he burst into gales of laughter. "You mean the Bargain Booking room? It's not much more than a broom closet, I know."

"Why didn't you tell me you booked us into the staff room?" Pete asked. "It cost a fortune. You could have got us a decent room."

The man slapped him on the shoulder. "I'm sorry. I know it's not much, but it's the best I could get you even at that price. The bigger rooms cost twice as much, and you said you wanted to keep costs down."

"I know, but....." Pete began.

The man waved his hand. "Never mind. You're here. That's what's important. Now introduce me to your lady friend or I'll start to suspect you're ashamed of me."

Pete gestured toward Vanessa. "This is Vanessa Abbot, Managing Director of the Harvest Home Cat Sanctuary. And this, Vanessa, is Robert Ipswich, my old nemesis, and manager of the Dove's Peak Ski Lodge."

Vanessa shook his hand. "It's a pleasure to meet you at last. I've heard so much about you."

Robert laughed again. "I'm sure Pete's told you

more about me than you ever wanted to know. Go on. He has. Admit it."

Vanessa turned red. "He has told me quite a lot about you."

He slapped his thigh. "I knew it! You can't keep the old skeletons in the closet."

Vanessa couldn't stop smiling. "Thank you so much for the room. It's perfect for us, and I'm certain we're going to have a weekend to remember."

"You are most welcome," Robert replied. "And if there is anything I can do to make your stay more enjoyable, please let me or Sally know. We're here to serve you. Now come on. The party's just getting started, and I want to introduce you to some people."

He led them into the midst of the celebration. He grabbed champagne glasses off the waiters' trays and shoved them into Pete and Vanessa's hands. He steered them toward the food and insisted they try everything in sight.

"And this is Brandon Groves," Robert told them. "He's an old friend of mine—but not as old a friend as you, Wheeler. He manages the Willow Brook Ski Lodge down the road. We're supposed to be in competition with each other, but we've always worked together to make the Dove's Peak ski area as popular as we can. When one of us benefits, we all benefit."

Brandon shook hands with Pete and Vanessa. He couldn't have been much older than Robert. "My pleasure."

"And don't forget," Robert went on, "I've

arranged for free ski equipment rentals for you both and free slope tickets, too. You won't have to pay anything more for your stay than your room fee."

"Thank you very much," Vanessa exclaimed. "I've never skied before, so Pete is going to teach me. That's why we decided to come up here."

Robert laughed. "Pete taught me how to drive a manual transmission, too."

"That was nice of him," Vanessa remarked.

Robert snorted. "It was very nice of him, but that's why I still drive an automatic."

The two friends laughed and elbowed each other until Sally came up to them. "I'm glad to see you two enjoying yourselves. I'd like to introduce you to my father, Frank. He's our local ski instructor, so if you take any lessons on the slopes, he's the best you can get."

Vanessa shook hands with Frank. He bowed his head to her, but he didn't smile. "I hope you won't be offended, but my friend Pete is going to teach me to ski."

Frank frowned. "You really should get a professional to teach you to ski. You don't want to have to unlearn bad habits later on. I have plenty of lesson time available this weekend. I would be happy to make time to show you the ropes."

Vanessa blushed. "I'm sure we'll be fine. Thank you anyway."

"Dad taught me to ski," Sally told her. "He used to be an Olympian."

"I was never an Olympian," Frank corrected

her. "I was in training for the Olympics when my career ended."

Vanessa pricked up her ears. "I'm sorry to hear that. What happened?"

Sally interrupted before her father could answer. "Dad taught me to ski. He's the best there is."

"I didn't teach you to ski," he countered. "You gave up before I had a chance."

"*You* gave up," Sally returned. "You got too frustrated with me, so you found one of your friends to take over my lessons. You never could reconcile yourself to the fact that I couldn't ski as well as you could."

Frank's expression softened. "That's true. I always wished you would take over where I left off."

A tidal wave of party-goers swept father and daughter into the crowd. Vanessa watched them disappear into the sea of heads. "Something's going on there."

Brandon spoke up. "You gotta feel bad for Frank, though."

"What happened to end his Olympic career?" Vanessa asked.

"A drunk driver plowed into his car and drove him off the road," Brandon replied. "He was hospitalized for weeks, and he never returned to competition."

"But he's the best ski instructor in the country," Robert added. "You can't do better than him."

Vanessa smiled and shook her head. "I'll stick

with Pete. He knows what he's doing."

An explosion of voices drew their attention toward the door. The crowd parted. Robert growled under his breath. "What's she doing here?"

An older woman broke through the crowd. Grey roots showed under her dyed black hair and diamond rings glittering on every finger. The party-goers retreated before her. A haze of alcohol blurred her wrinkled eyes. Vanessa took a step back. "Who is that?"

"It's Joan Pritchett," Robert told her. "She inherited the lodge from her family, but she can't be bothered with the responsibility of ownership. She's never here, and when she does show up, she causes more trouble than she's worth. She should stay away, especially from staff functions. She makes everyone uncomfortable."

Joan stalked into the room on her spike-heeled shoes. The party-goers turned their backs on her and tried to ignore her. Joan grabbed a champagne glass and headed for the center of the room. Her footsteps echoed off the ceiling.

In the center of the hall, she cut her hand across her neck and the music died. "I want to thank all of you for your hard work over the years. You all have made this lodge the success it is."

Vanessa leaned toward Pete. "She's drunk."

Robert smacked his lips. "She always is. She's too inebriated to know what she's saying."

"I have a special announcement to make to you all tonight." A hush fell over the crowd. "The Dove's Peak Ski Lodge will officially close down next year and be converted into timeshare properties. I'm sure all of you will go on to even greater successes in your various careers. Each and every one of you is responsible for bringing the lodge to this success with guests coming from all over the country, and I want to thank you from the bottom of my heart. I will be happy to provide letters of recommendation for everyone."

A murmur of alarm ran through the crowd. Brandon stepped forward and jabbed at Joan with his finger. "You're a heartless snake, Joan. I would never have believed that you could stoop as low as this."

Joan's bejeweled hand flew to her heart. "Why, whatever do you mean?"

"The Dove's Peak Lodge was never your success at all," Brandon told her. "Your family bought this lodge when Dove's Peak was a small mountain town community, and it's always been about the close-knit community coming back here year after year. Now you're destroying that because you don't have the brains to run it as a business. Timeshares will only bring in more tourists who don't care about the town, and you'll be long gone with your money. You should be ashamed of yourself."

Joan fixed him with a vicious glare. "This party is for Dove's Peak staff, and you're manager of a competing ski lodge. You shouldn't even be here."

Robert came to Brandon's side. "I invited Brandon to this party, and he has more right to be here than you do, Joan. This is a doozy of a way to fire your whole staff, at their staff party, but I should know better than to expect anything else from you. You're a spineless snake in the grass, and you always have been."

Joan swept the company with her eyes. She must have known she had no friends in that crowd. "I might be a spineless snake, but I'm still in charge here. Make sure this party's over by ten o'clock. We still have paying guests here. You don't want to disturb anybody, do you?"

A young woman with flaming red hair stepped out from behind the bar. "What are you going to do to us if we don't close down the party by ten? You can't fire us. It's too late for that."

Frank Bendall came to her side. "You've dropped your bomb, Joan. Now go back to your room and let us finish our party."

Joan opened her mouth, but the plain hatred of everyone surrounding her made her close it again. She glared at the crowd one last time and stamped out of the room. The noise from her shoe heels died on the carpet in the main lobby, and the door banged shut.

The red-headed bartender picked up a tray of champagne glasses and handed them around. "This will be the last *End of Season* Party, so you might as well drink up and enjoy yourselves."

Sally turned to Vanessa. "This is Tiffany Harley. This is her first *End of Season* Party, and now it's going to be her last, too. She moved here from San Francisco to start a new life."

Tiffany smiled. "I'll start a new life, all right. I'll just start it somewhere else."

"You come over to the Willow Brook, Tiffany," Brandon told her. "I'll give you a job."

Tiffany shook her head. "I don't think so. I think I'll go overseas. I still have the rest of the world to see before I get too old to enjoy myself."

Robert tipped his champagne glass up to this mouth and choked. "Tiffany! You could get....."

Tiffany threw back her head. "I could get what? I could get fired? I just got fired. I can't get fired twice.."

"What's going on?" Vanessa asked.

"Taste the champagne," Pete told her.

"How did you get your hands on this? Do you know how much this cost per bottle?" Robert asked. "You shouldn't have done this, Tiffany."

"I broke into the store room to get the good stuff," Tiffany explained. "Now none of us have to worry about getting into trouble with Joan. Let's all raise our glasses and toast the fact that we never have to work for that troll again."

Robert took a tentative sip of his champagne. "I'm glad I don't have to work for Joan anymore, but I'm sorry this is the last year the lodge will be in operation. It's a terrible waste."

"Joan's had everything handed to her in her life," Brandon replied. "She doesn't value anything or anybody."

Robert nodded. "She had a wild and crazy youth. If her father hadn't bailed her out more than once, she probably would have ended up in prison."

"Her father built this lodge from nothing," Brandon told them. "He was a true businessman."

"And now he's dead, and Joan inherited it from him," Robert went on. "She's been coming here all her life, and she never liked this place. I don't think she set foot on the slopes or even outside the doors in winter. She hates cold and wet, and she never did anything active in her life. Now's her chance never to have to come back here again."

"That's a shame," Vanessa exclaimed.

Robert jumped up on a table. He raised his champagne glass above his head. "I'll tell you one thing that's not a shame, though. I have never been so proud to work with such a fine group of people. I can't tell you all how grateful I am to work with each and every person here, and you know I don't mean that the way Joan does. I'll do everything in my power to make sure you find good jobs after this, and I know you'll do as well in the future as you've done here. So let's raise our glasses and toast—to us!"

The crowd raised their glasses in unison, and the shout echoed to the skies. "To us!"

CHAPTER 3

❖

A scream awakened Vanessa out of a sound sleep. Pete's face peered down from the top bunk. His hair stood out from his head, and his mustache stuck out from his face. He rubbed his eyes. "Did you hear something?"

"It sounded like a scream," she told him.

He rolled out of the bunk and landed on his feet on the floor. "I'll check it out."

"You can't go in your pajamas," Vanessa reminded him.

He stopped with his hand on the doorknob and glanced down at his pajamas. "Oh. Right."

After he changed and left to investigate, Vanessa

dug herself out from under her cats. "Move over, Flossy. You always hog the whole bed to yourself. Move over, Henry. Man, you're heavy! You really need to go on a diet."

She put on her bathrobe and found three cans of cat food in her suitcase.

"I know I always say that," Vanessa went on. "It's true, isn't it? Maggie said you were overweight a dozen times before Sam took over, and now he's saying the same thing. Don't gloat, Flossy. You're no lightweight yourself. Sam is right. I'm just too soft on you cats. You need a vet taking care of you."

She served three servings of cat food into three separate dishes. Flossy and Aurora hopped off the bed and gobbled their food while Henry watched from the bed through narrowed eyes. Vanessa plugged in the electric coffee pot.

"No, I don't plan to turn over the Sanctuary to Sam Powell," she told him. "Whatever gave you an idea like that? You know as well as anybody, Henry. This is the first weekend away I've taken in almost twenty years, and I couldn't even be persuaded to leave you three at home. That just goes to show how dedicated I am to you cats."

Henry narrowed his eyes and flicked his tail.

Vanessa snorted. "You're right. I should take more vacations but that still doesn't mean Sam is going to take over the Sanctuary. He plans to go into private practice in Caspar Crossing, and when Maggie retires to the racing circuit, he'll have all the work he can handle. With his personality and work ethic, he should be very successful."

She sat down on the bed with her coffee cup. Henry looked back and forth between Vanessa and the other cats wolfing their food.

"That Joan Pritchett," she murmured. "She's a bad one. I don't think I've ever seen a worse specimen than that. You should have seen her at that party last night. She was bleary-eyed drunk, but she still managed to exude an air of ruthless hostility toward everyone in the place. I don't even know her, and even I started to hate her. And then when she made that announcement about the lodge closing down and all the staff being out on their ears, I could understand why no one wants her around."

Flossy licked her lips and meowed up at Vanessa.

"No, Flossy, dear," Vanessa told her. "Stop whining. That's all the food you get for now. The answer is no."

Aurora jumped back on the bed and cleaned her paws. Henry waited until Flossy moved away from the food dishes and Vanessa picked up the two empty ones before he hopped down and moved toward his food.

I'm telling you, Henry," Vanessa went on, "she gave the staff the news at their party just to hurt their feelings. She could have let them enjoy themselves for one night before she dropped her bomb—but no! She had to gatecrash the staff party just to tell them they were all out of a job. I've never experienced anything so rude in my life."

Henry bent over his dish and ate.

"You don't understand," Vanessa told him. "The Dove's Peak Ski Lodge became successful by fostering a community of loyal guests who keep coming back year after year from all over the world. Joan deliberately set out to ruin that with her timeshare plan. I don't know what these people are going to do."

Henry finished eating and sat up.

Vanessa stared down at him with her coffee cup resting on her knee. "Of course, they'll get new jobs. That's not the point."

Pete came back and shut the door behind him. "You won't believe it. Joan Pritchett is dead."

Vanessa whirled around so fast she startled the cats. "Dead!"

Pete nodded. "Murdered. That scream came from the maid. She found Joan's body under the balcony of her room when she emptied the vacuum canister into the dumpster."

Vanessa gasped. "Is there any evidence of how

it happened?"

"There's no sign of forced entry," Pete replied. "But the room door was found unlocked, and one of Joan's false fingernails came loose. I found scuffmarks on the frame of the sliding door leading out to the balcony. Someone went to Joan's room last night, and after she had opened the door to let them in, they struggled. Then the person pushed her over the rail, and she fell to her death."

"Who would do such a thing?" Vanessa asked.

Pete shrugged and squeezed himself next to Flossy on the bottom bunk. "It must have been someone Joan knew well enough to let into her room in the first place."

"Maybe it was one of the lodge staff," Vanessa suggested. "Maybe it was one of the cleaners or room service staff."

From what I saw last night," Pete replied, "lots of people had a motive to kill Joan."

Vanessa dropped her spoon and tore off her bathrobe. "I'm going to find out more."

Pete stopped her with his hand on her arm. "Let the local police handle this. A detective from the police station showed up at the same time I did. I left when he started to investigate."

Vanessa rounded on him. "What? Do you mean you aren't going to investigate? What's wrong with you?"

"This isn't my jurisdiction," he told her. "I'm here on vacation. The local detective can handle it as well as I can. I'm going to relax and take you skiing. I don't want to get involved."

Vanessa pulled on her pants and tied her shoes. "I know we're here to relax, but it won't hurt to pass by the crime scene. I just want to look. I won't interfere with the investigation."

Pete chuckled and shook his head. "You're hopeless, aren't you? All right, we'll go, and then we're heading out to the slopes."

A crowd gathered under Joan's balcony. Three uniformed police officers blocked off a perimeter of cordon tape to keep the crowd back. Vanessa elbowed her way through the crowd to the barrier, where a detective in a suit took notes on his phone. "What happened here?"

The detective looked up. "Can I help you, Ma'am?"

Vanessa glanced at the badge stuck into his

lapel pocket. "Detective Phil Maskey. I'm Vanessa Abbot."

He studied her with his stern blue eyes. Grey hair showed under his hat. "What can I do for you, Ms. Abbot?"

"I was just wondering what happened here," she told him.

Detective Maskey glanced over Vanessa's shoulder. Pete flashed the detective his badge. The detective nodded. "We're investigating a murder. That's what happened here."

"Were there any witnesses?" she asked.

"If there were any witnesses," he replied, "we wouldn't have to investigate. The only witness is another guest who heard voices arguing in Ms. Pritchett's room last night. The guest didn't report it, so it must not have been anything serious. Then, this morning, the maid found Ms. Pritchett's body under the balcony. We're treating it as a homicide. That's what happened here."

"Whoever was arguing with her must be the killer," Vanessa remarked. "Could the witness tell whether Joan was arguing with a man or a woman?"

The detective shook his head. "Couldn't make out a thing. It sounded muffled behind the wall. The argument didn't last long, and when it ended, she assumed everything was all right. Then she went to bed."

Pete stepped forward and laid his hand on Vanessa's arm. "Detective Maskey will handle the investigation from here. Let's get out to the slopes. We only have a few days to enjoy ourselves before it's time to leave."

Vanessa nodded. "Thank you for your help, Detective Maskey."

He bobbed the brim of his hat to her. "Anything to oblige, and you can call me Phil."

Vanessa smiled. "Thank you, Phil."

Pete and Vanessa stopped by the rental shop, and the technician fitted Vanessa with skis, boots, and poles. Then they lugged their gear out to the ski fields. Vanessa stumbled when she tried to walk in her heavy ski boots, but she couldn't hold her skis and poles in one arm and hold onto the railing for balance with the other. When she tried, she dropped her skis, and when she picked them up and carried them with both arms, the boots made her stumble.

Pete didn't notice. He slotted his skis together somehow and slung them over his shoulder. He carried both poles in his other hand and clomped out of the rental shop. Once outside, Vanessa shielded her eyes from the sun glaring off the snow. The chairlift sailed over her head. "How do we get up there?"

"We don't get up there," he told her. "When you're just learning, you stay on the bunny slopes."

"The bunny slopes?" she asked. "What's that?"

Pete pointed to a gentle incline between the chairlift and the lodge door. Kids on metal dishes and broken cardboard boxes skidded down the slope and crashed into the lodge steps. "That's the bunny slope. That's where you learn how to ski. Until you master that, there's no point in you going anywhere else, especially not up the chairlift."

Vanessa cast a wistful glance at people in slick ski suits swishing down the slopes and throwing up sprays of snow when they skidded to a stop next to the lift. They made it look so easy, and their designer suits and sunglasses made skiing all the more glamorous.

"I'm sure I'll master it in no time," she told Pete. "Then you can show me the higher slopes."

Pete held up his hand. "One step at a time. You've got your boots on, so put on your skis."

Vanessa set her skis on the ground, but when she tried to step into the bindings, she almost fell over. Pete caught her by the arm. "Careful."

She tried again and twisted her ankle. Then she fell over and buried her knee in the snow. Freezing cold water soaked through her pant leg. By the time she pushed herself up into a standing position again, her hands were shaking with cold.

"Watch me," Pete told her. "Set your ski poles on the ground like this and use them to balance yourself. Stick the toe of your boot into the front of the binding. Then step down hard on the back piece and make it lock over your heel—like this."

She watched him lock his boot into his bindings and copied him, but the thing spat her out and tipped her over again. Pete steadied her by holding onto her arm. When she fell over the third time, she smacked her lips and shook him off. "Let me go. You're only making it harder."

He threw up his hands and turned his back on her while she kicked and struggled to get her skis locked into place. She got the first one locked, but when she tried to step into the second one, the ski on her other foot slipped on the snow, and she went down on one knee again. This time, though, she didn't bother to stand up. She dug her knee into the snow and forced her foot into the binding.

She panted from the effort and pushed herself to her feet with her ski poles. Staying upright took all her balance. Pete still stood with his back to her. "I'm ready now."

He turned around and scanned her up and down. "Good. Come on."

He shoved off with his poles and glided along the path toward the top of the bunny slope. Vanessa hesitated. "How are we supposed to get up there?"

"Just push yourself along—like this," he called back.

She pushed off—and crashed in a heap of skis,

poles and flailing limbs. In a fit of spite, she tore off her skis and walked up the hill, where she went through the laborious operation of putting her skis on all over again. Pete watched with a touch of a smile on his face, but he didn't say anything.

When at last she stood ready at the top of the bunny slope, Pete shoved off one more time and inched down the hill. "Just copy me, and whatever you do, keep your skis straight."

She dug in her poles, and her skis slipped over the snow. In an instant, her skis crossed at the front tips. She tried to correct, but they slid out of her control. They crossed at right angles to each other, and her legs crossed over one another. In another moment, her legs went in opposite directions.

"Keep your skis straight!" Pete yelled.

But it was too late. She tumbled onto the snow in a hopeless tangle. While she was still trying to extricate herself from the mess, Pete's face appeared over her. "Why didn't you keep your skis straight?"

She glared at him with gritted teeth. "I am keeping them straight. What do you think I'm doing?"

He pursed his lips. "Listen. I'm just trying to help you. If you can't follow simple instructions, you'll never learn to ski."

Vanessa ripped off her skis and unclipped her boots. She threw them into the snow and tossed her ski poles down on top of them. "I don't want to learn to ski. I'm going back to the room."

Pete threw up his hands. "Oh, come on! It isn't as bad as that. Just give it one more try. Don't give up now. It's not that hard."

Vanessa didn't answer, and she didn't look at him, either. She turned her back on him and stomped back to the lodge through the snow in her socks.

Her feet ached with cold by the time she got there, but she brightened up when she found Sally sitting on the steps. Henry stood at her feet, and Sally ran her hand down the tabby cat's back.

"Hello, Henry. Did you make a new friend?" Vanessa asked.

Sally looked up. "Do you know this cat?"

Vanessa nodded. "He's my cat. He's supposed to be staying in the room, but somehow he always manages to find a way out. He has a sixth sense for that."

Sally smiled down at Henry, and he rubbed against her shins. "He's been comforting me."

Vanessa cocked her head. "Do you need comforting?"

Sally nodded. "The police have questioned everyone at the lodge about Joan's death. That detective said Joan was murdered, and we're all suspects. Everyone's on edge because.....well, the fact is we all did want her dead."

"I suppose none of you has an alibi," Vanessa remarked.

Sally shook her head. "After the party, everyone went back to their rooms. No one saw anything."

Vanessa rubbed her chin. "What about you? Did you go back to your room after the party?"

"I have my own room at the back of the lodge,"

Sally explained. "I live alone because I'm the Concierge. No one can vouch for my whereabouts after I left the party."

"Do you have any idea who might have killed Joan?" Vanessa asked.

"It could have been anyone," Sally replied. "Everybody hated Joan, and after she made that announcement about shutting down the lodge, every employee had a motive."

Just then, Flossy stuck her head out of a snow bank. She pounced after a cardinal pecking breadcrumbs around the picnic tables. Sally stared at her. "What a beautiful cat! I don't think I've ever seen so many cats around the lodge before."

Vanessa blushed. "That is also my cat."

Sally's eyes popped open. "How many do you

have?"

Vanessa closed her eyes and laughed. "I run a cat sanctuary. But I only brought three on this vacation. We'll probably see the other one in a few minutes."

Sally scratched Henry behind the ears. "They're wonderful cats. I wish I had a cat."

"I'm sure I could help you out with that," Vanessa replied. "I run a Cat Sanctuary in Caspar Crossing. People bring me abandoned and unwanted cats all the time, and I'm always looking for homes for them. If you are interested, I could set you to adopt one."

Sally's head shot up. "Could you, really? That would be wonderful! I would love a cat."

Vanessa smiled down at her. "I would be

honored. Any cat lover is a friend of mine."

Sally looked around. "Where's your friend—the one that was going to teach you to ski?"

Vanessa waved her hand. "He's over there enjoying himself on the slopes without me. He tried to teach me to ski, but it ended in disaster. Now I'm on my way back to our room."

Sally nodded. "You should never take ski lessons from loved ones. I learned that the hard way with my dad. He tried to teach me to ski, and that ended in disaster, too. I had to learn from someone else."

Vanessa frowned. "Maybe I should learn from someone else, too."

"Take a lesson from my dad," Sally told her. "You two don't know each other, and he's the best there is. He's very patient with beginners—as long as they aren't related to him, and I know he has some free lesson time available this afternoon."

Vanessa smiled. "Okay. That sounds perfect."

Sally stood up. "I'll find him and arrange it."

"Thank you, Sally." She picked up Flossy in one arm and Henry in the other. "Come on, you rascals. It's time to go back to the room."

She set them down on the bunk bed and closed the door. Then she put out their food. She petted Henry while Flossy and Aurora ate. "Where have you cats been all day?"

Flossy kept her nose stuck in her dish. Aurora sneezed and shook food crumbs off her whiskers.

"I tried to investigate Joan's death, too," Vanessa told them, "but between the police and Pete Wheeler, I couldn't get anywhere close to the crime scene. They've cooked up a conspiracy to make me relax. Even Pete had turned his back on the investigation. He says the local detective can handle it. That's not like him at all."

Henry stretched out on the bed next to her and purred.

Vanessa picked up Flossy and Aurora's dishes and put out Henry's, but he didn't move. "I know he's on vacation. I'm on vacation, too. But that doesn't mean I can't be curious about a mysterious murder. I would have to have my head examined if I didn't."

Henry closed his eyes and turned away.

"Don't tell me you don't want to investigate this murder, Henry?" she asked him. "You heard Sally Bendall. The whole lodge is in an uproar about it, and everyone at the staff party is a suspect."

Henry jumped off the bed and sniffed his food dish. He closed his eyes and turned away.

"I thought the same thing," Vanessa told him. "I don't suspect Sally either, but I don't want to get ahead of myself. We need to find out more about what happened in Joan's room."

Henry took the first taste of his food. Aurora and Flossy climbed into the top bunk and curled up together.

"I brought you cats here to enjoy the snow," Vanessa told them, "remember this is your vacation too."

Henry looked over his shoulder up at Vanessa.

Vanessa smiled. "Just be careful if you head out into the lodge. If you find out anything about this murder, be sure to let me know right away."

CHAPTER 4

❖

Frank Bendall stopped by turning his skis sideways and sprayed snow into the air. Vanessa pointed her skis inward and braked to a stop next to him. He smiled for the first time since she met him. "Good work. You're getting good at stopping."

Vanessa smiled, too. "It's not as hard as I thought. I think I'm getting the hang of it."

He pointed to the top of the chairlift. "How would you like to take a crack at the beginner slope?"

Vanessa narrowed her eyes at the top of the hill. "Up there? Do you think I'm ready for it?"

He skated toward the chairlift. "That's what

it's there for. If anything gets in your way, you just turn. It's easy, and I'll be with you all the way." He sidestepped into line with the other skiers waiting for the lift.

Vanessa took a deep breath. "All right. What could possibly go wrong?"

He grinned. "That's the spirit."

In a moment, Frank and Vanessa sat side by side in the chairlift. They soared over skiers on the slope and up the hill into the great beyond. "You're a great instructor, Frank. I can't believe I'm taking a lesson from someone who almost competed in the Olympics."

Frank shrugged. "I have spent a lifetime on these slopes."

"I can see you love what you do," she replied.

"You have a natural ability to inspire confidence, and confidence is what you need to ski."

He studied her. "You should forgive your friend Pete. He did his best to teach you, and there's nothing harder than trying to teach someone you love. I learned that trying to coach Sally, and she was a really good skier."

"Did you tell her that?" Vanessa asked. "I don't think she knows. She thinks she never lived up to your expectations, and you set the bar pretty high by being the best of the best."

He grimaced. "I should tell her. I know she's suffered all these years thinking she's not as good as me when in fact she's every bit as good as I ever was. The friend I asked to teach her for me said so, too."

"What about Sally's mother?" Vanessa asked. "Did you teach her to ski, too?"

Frank burst out laughing. "Her? No one on earth could teach her to ski."

Vanessa's eyes widened. "Why?"

Frank finished chuckling. "My wife Roxanne was a wonderful mother, but she never learned to ski. I tried to teach her once—only once—and that was the last time. She tried taking lessons from other people, too, but she eventually gave up." He gazed into the distance. "I can't tell you how hard it was raising Sally after she died. No one can understand that who hasn't been through it."

Vanessa gasped. "I didn't know Sally's mother had passed away. I'm sorry to bring it up."

"No need to apologize," he replied.

"My husband died years ago, too," Vanessa told him. "I have been through the same experience, and I understand how hard it is. I still miss him every day. I wish he'd been around to help me raise my son Tom."

Frank smiled. "That's exactly how I feel. It's nice to know I'm not alone in the world."

The chairlift zoomed around its top pulley, and Frank helped Vanessa ski out of it. They made their way to the top of the beginner slope. "Are you ready for this?"

Vanessa gazed down the hill. "There's no time like the present."

She squared her shoulders and pushed off. She kept her skis straight and sped down the hill, faster and faster. The lodge grew up large in front of her.

She threw back her head and let the wind blow through her hair. For a fraction of an instant, she could have spread her arms and launched herself into the air like a bird on the wing.

All of a sudden, her left ski wobbled. Her shoulders tightened, and her attention reverted to doing everything Frank told her to do. She concentrated all her might on keeping her skis straight, but she couldn't get them to track the right way. She started to drift to her left toward the trees and rocks.

Frank shouted to her from behind. "Weave back and forth to slow down."

But she was going too fast. She teetered on one ski, and when she put the other one down next to it, they started to cross in front of her. She fought to gain control, but every bump threatened to knock her off her feet.

Frank skied down next to her and rode at her side. He inched closer, and she automatically corrected to put some distance between them. Inch by inch, he moved her away from the trees. She slowed down enough to regain control of her skis and her legs. He veered right toward the center of the slope, and she matched him with a sigh of relief. The next minute, they both skidded to a stop at the bottom of the slope.

Vanessa beamed. "Thanks."

He grinned and nodded up the hill. "Want to try another run?"

Vanessa shook her head. "I think I'll get a hot chocolate instead."

They separated at the entrance to the chairlift.

Frank waved to her before he rode up to the advanced slopes, and Vanessa went back to the lodge. She stacked her skis and poles in the rack by the door and tromped into the lobby in her ski boots. She smiled to herself and held her head high. She was a skier now, just like all the other glamorous people at Dove's Peak. She might not be as glamorous as they were, but at least now she could ski. When Pete came back, she would be ready to ski with him on the slopes.

She got her hot chocolate from the cafe and took it back to her room. Henry sat up on the bed when she walked in, and Flossy opened her eyes and meowed. Vanessa hung her ski jacket on the bedpost and kicked off her ski boots. She sat down on the bed next to Henry with a satisfied sigh. "You won't believe it. I'm a skier."

Henry curled up again. He tucked his paws under his chest and closed his eyes. The wind whistled through a crack in the window frame.

Vanessa smiled at him. "So you didn't think I would go through with it, huh? Well, I did. I got lessons from Frank."

Henry's ear twitched. He wrapped his tail around his body and covered his eyes with it. Vanessa stretched out on the bed next to him and stroked his fur. She arranged her feet so as not to disturb Flossy and Aurora.

"What have you been doing today?" Vanessa told Henry. "I saw you and Flossy running around outside. Did you investigate the murder scene? I'd bet good money you cats have seen more of this lodge than I have."

Her stroking hand disturbed Henry's rest. He brought his head up and pretended to bite her, but she ignored him.

"That's true. There were no signs that the door was kicked in. The killer was obviously someone she knew. She let them into the room and then they began to fight," Vanessa went on. "I can understand that the entire staff would be upset. Frank might have wanted to protect his daughter from losing her job. Or Sally wanted to save her Dad's job? Tiffany seemed ready to give Joan a piece of her mind. I was surprised Brandon seemed so angry. I understand he loves this community but is it enough to kill someone over? Whoever confronted her that night, let it get out of control and Joan ended up falling to her death."

Henry fixed her with his green eyes and lashed the blanket with his tail.

"I know she couldn't have fallen over the railing by accident," Vanessa told him. "Don't you remember Pete telling us they found signs of a struggle in the room? She fought her attacker off. I'm surprised the lady next door didn't hear screaming."

Henry licked his chops and looked the other way.

Vanessa chuckled and started rubbing her lower back. "Yes, you are probably right. A day on the slopes is going to wear anyone out. I wouldn't be surprised if the woman next door was sleeping through the whole ordeal."

Flossy stood up, walked in a circle around Aurora, and coiled herself around the kitten again.

"What did you see, Flossy?" Vanessa watched her. "Robert was with a woman with red hair behind the lodge? That may have been Tiffany. She works as the bartender. They might have been going over inventory."

Flossy licked Aurora's ear, and the kitten started to purr.

"They were whispering and looking around? That does sound suspicious. I wonder if there is more going on between them," Vanessa yawned. "I will find out more tonight at dinner."

Vanessa put her head on the pillow, and a wave of exhaustion washed over her. The effort of skiing hit her like a ton of bricks, and she couldn't keep her eyes open. Her hand went still on Henry's back, and silence descended over the room. Not even the steaming hot chocolate could rouse her. She sank into the bed and fell fast asleep.

CHAPTER 5

❖

Vanessa's eyes fluttered open. The cats hadn't moved, but the sun had moved around to the other side of the building. She sat up and checked the clock. It was past five in the afternoon. She ran her fingers through her hair and got out of the bunk.

Henry blinked at her, and Flossy sat up to clean her paws. Aurora still quivered in her dreams at the end of the bed. Vanessa peeled off her ski suit, opened her suitcase, and took out her evening suit.

She held it up and brushed a speck of lint off it. She hung it on the upper bunk when the door opened. Pete Wheeler came in and smiled at her. He took a package from under his arm and handed her a present wrapped in snowflake wrapping paper with a huge white bow on top. "This is for you."

Vanessa gasped and kissed him on the cheek. "You didn't have to give me anything."

He sat down on the bunk and scratched Flossy behind the ears. "Don't thank me until you've seen it. The gift shop isn't much to write home about."

Vanessa tore into the package and took out a striped scarf and a snow globe with a snowman inside it. She held them up and laughed. "Thank you. I love them both." She kissed him again.

He leaned back against the bedpost. "I saw you on the slopes with Frank. You're making good progress."

Vanessa sat down next to him and took his

hand. "I'm sorry I made a stink when you tried to teach me. I should have been more patient."

He kissed her hand. "That was my fault. Let's forget all about it and enjoy the rest of the weekend."

Vanessa smoothed her suit again. "I was just getting ready for dinner."

"Robert and Brandon invited us to join them," Pete told her.

"That was nice of them," Vanessa remarked.

"If I know Robert Ipswich," Pete replied, "he's up to something."

"You don't think he's planning another one of his jokes, do you?" Vanessa asked.

"He's always planning something," Pete told

him. "I've known him longer than anybody. He wouldn't have invited us if he wasn't planning something."

"Maybe he just wants to spend time with his old friend," Vanessa suggested.

Pete snorted. "Yeah. He wants to rile me up the way he used to in college."

Vanessa stared at him. "How does he do that?"

Pete shrugged. "He has known me long enough to know what buttons to push. You can't trust that guy any farther than you can throw him."

Vanessa laughed. "If I know you at all, I'll bet you riled him up plenty of times, too. I'd say you gave as good as you got."

Pete's eyes popped open. "What? Me? Your knight in shining armor?"

Vanessa laughed. "Don't think you can pull the wool over my eyes with that innocent act. I know you, Pete Wheeler, and I've seen the way your mind turns when you talk about Robert pulling pranks on you. You two were partners in crime back in college, and you haven't lost your trickster nature. It might have gone underground when you joined the police force, but it's been waiting for a chance to come back out and wreak havoc. You getting back together with Robert Ipswich could be just the chance you're looking for."

Pete frowned. "I swear, I don't know what you're talking about, Your Honor. I never planned a prank in my life. I never had anything to do with Robert Ipswich or his devious adventures."

Vanessa chucked him on the arm. "Come on and get dressed. We don't want to keep them waiting."

Pete escorted Vanessa to the dining hall. Robert waved them over to his table. Brandon sat across from them. "Sit down, sit down. I've been waiting for you two for ages. I have your favorite drink ready for you, Wheeler."

Pete stared at a tumbler on the table filled with amber liquid. "An Old Fashioned!" He burst out laughing. "I haven't had a cocktail like this in years."

Robert held the glass out to him. "Then you've got a lot of catching up to do. No one makes a better Old Fashioned than Tiffany."

Pete and Vanessa sat down with Robert and Brandon, and Pete sipped his drink. Robert flagged down the nearest waiter. "How did the lesson go?"

Pete almost choked on his drink, and Vanessa

turned bright red. "It went perfectly. I learned how to ski from Frank Bendall."

Robert stared at her. Brandon nodded. "Frank's the best there is. I've known him since we were kids. We both grew up in this Dove's Peak, and we practically learned to ski before we learned to walk."

"Was that before the lodge opened?" Vanessa asked.

Brandon nodded. "Before old Mr. Pritchett, Joan's father owned this place, Doves' Peak was a small, tight community. After a snowstorm, you could ski down Main Street, and wave to everyone as you passed. Kids skied until dark, and then they skied home. That's how safe it was."

"It sounds wonderful," Vanessa exclaimed.

Brandon nodded. "I miss those days, but I guess they'll never come again. After Joan's father bought the land and opened the lodge, most of the original residents moved out, and the community fell apart."

Vanessa caught sight of Frank at the bar. "There's Frank. Would you excuse me? I want to thank him for the lesson."

Frank and Sally murmured to each other over drinks at the bar, but they separated when Vanessa approached. "I hope I'm not interrupting anything."

Sally set down her empty glass. "Not at all. I was just going back to work."

"I want to thank you again, Frank, for rescuing me on the slopes," Vanessa told him. "I would have been in the hospital now if it wasn't for you."

He shrugged. "It's all part of the job. Besides, you should give yourself more credit. You're getting to be a good skier. You have a natural ability."

Vanessa waved her hand. "I don't think so."

Tiffany called to Vanessa over the bar. "Can I get you anything?"

"I'd like to buy another round of drinks for Frank and Sally," Vanessa replied, "and a glass of wine for me."

Tiffany moved down the bar to pour Frank's drink. Framed photographs lined the back of the bar.

"Who are all those people?" Vanessa asked.

"They're members of the lodge," Frank replied.

"That gallery dates back to the first years the Pritchett family owned this place. That's Joan and her family in the center of each one."

Vanessa took a closer look. "Brandon is in them, too. He's got his arm around Joan in every picture."

"He used to date her back then," Frank told her.

"And he disappears in that picture there." Vanessa squinted across the bar. "1987. That's strange. Joan's not in any of the pictures after that, either. What happened?"

"They broke up," Frank replied. "Afterward, Joan went away to school in Europe. She never came back for the photo again. She never came back at all until after her father died and she inherited the lodge. She tried to manage the place, but she had no business sense at all. Robert saved the place from bankruptcy."

"Do you know why she and Brandon broke up?" Vanessa asked.

Frank made a face. "Joan always thought Brandon was a townie. He was always happy here and didn't want to leave, and she had her sights set on bigger things. She made nasty comments about him right to his face—in public, even. I don't know why he stuck with her as long as he did."

"He must really have loved her," Vanessa remarked.

Frank turned away. "I think he was just interested in her money."

Tiffany brought over two pints of beer and set a wine glass in front of Vanessa. Sally raised her glass. "Here's to you, Dad, the hero of the slopes."

Vanessa joined in, "Here, here." They clinked their glasses together, and even Frank smiled.

He set his half-empty beer glass on the bar. "Excuse me a moment, will you?"

Vanessa watched him head toward the bathroom. "He's a great guy. Do you hang out with your dad much?"

Sally took a step closer and lowered her voice. "We've just been celebrating."

"Celebrating what?" Vanessa asked.

"Dad just told me the good news," Sally replied. "The lodge is staying open after all."

Vanessa's eyes popped open. "What?"

Sally nodded. "Joan never signed the final

papers selling the Dove's Peak to the timeshare developers. The lodge is safe."

"Wow," Vanessa exclaimed. "That's great for you, isn't it? When did your dad find out?"

"This morning," Sally replied. "He was more worried about me losing my job than anything else, so when he found out, he wanted to set my mind at ease. That's the kind of guy he is, always thinking of others."

"What about you?" Vanessa asked. "Were you worried about losing your job?"

"Everyone was," Sally replied. "I wasn't as worried as some. I can always get another job. There are enough other ski resorts in the area, and they're always hiring anyone with experience. Some of the managers of other lodges have offered me jobs before. I'm sure I wouldn't lose any time getting one."

Vanessa gazed across the room. "There's always the Willow Brook Ski Lodge. I'm sure Brandon would give you a job."

Sally smiled. "He's one of the managers who already has. I've only stayed at the Dove's Peak Lodge because my dad's here."

"Maybe Brandon would give him a job, too," Vanessa replied.

Sally nodded. "Dad could get a job anywhere. He never worried about himself when Joan made her announcement. He could even freelance as a ski instructor or even start his own business."

Just then, Robert shouted and waved to Vanessa across the dining room. "Come quick! You have to hear this story."

Vanessa touched her wine glass to Sally's beer. "I better go. Thanks again for setting up that lesson for me with your dad."

"It was my pleasure," Sally replied.

"I'll see you soon." Vanessa strolled back to the table and sat down next to Pete.

"I was just telling the story about when Pete and I got arrested," Robert told her.

Vanessa gasped. "Arrested!"

Robert slapped his thigh and laughed. "Someone dared us to sneak into the college pool. We would have gotten away with it if the security guard hadn't decided to go for a swim at the same time. We had to wait six hours in the holding cell in our wet swim trunks for our parents to bail us out."

Pete turned bright red and ran his finger around the rim of his glass.

"I didn't know you were an outlaw before you joined the force," Vanessa told him.

Pete snuck a peek at her face. Then he burst into a grin. "I was the worst criminal the town ever saw.

CHAPTER 6

❖

Vanessa knocked snow off her snowshoes with her ski poles. Then she hitched her backpack up on her shoulders. Henry stuck his head out through the top flap and meowed. "Don't worry," Vanessa told him. "We'll stop soon and then you can get out."

Pete scanned the snow-covered trees. "This is a good spot. Let's stop here."

He unfastened his snowshoes from his boots and stuck them in a snow bank next to the path. Vanessa unslung her pack and opened the flap. All three cats sprang out and scampered through the snow. "Don't run off!"

Pete chuckled. "They won't go anywhere. Let

them play for a while. This is the first time they've been out of the room since we got here."

"Don't kid yourself," Vanessa replied. "I caught Henry and Flossy running around near the ski slopes and getting cozy with the locals. They've also been investigating the murder scene. I'm sure they were sneaking out as soon as I turned my back."

"How else are they going to enjoy their vacation?" Pete asked.

Vanessa took sandwiches, a flask of hot chocolate, and a plastic box of fruit salad out of her pack. She hunted around and brought out a packet of cat food for the cats. She spread a blanket on the snow and sat down. "Sally told me last night the lodge is staying open after all. Joan never made the sale final, so her plan to sell out to developers has fallen through."

Pete stopped eating. "Robert must be relieved."

"I'm sure a lot of people are relieved," Vanessa replied. "I'm sure no one is as relieved as the killer."

"What's that supposed to mean?" he asked.

"I mean the killer's motive for killing Joan was successful," she explained. "They stopped the sale, and now the lodge is staying open, just like they wanted it to."

Pete nodded. "That's true. I wonder who was going to be the most effected by this sale."

An ear-splitting yowl startled them both. Vanessa dropped her sandwich. She spun around just in time to see all three cats dive under the backpack flap and hide inside. "What's gotten into them?"

Before she could answer, Vanessa choked on

her fruit salad. Pete pointed back the way they came. "Look at that."

A giant plume of black smoke rose above the trees. The wail of sirens echoed through the woods. "What's going on?"

Pete stepped into his snowshoes. "It's coming from the lodge. Come on. We have to get back."

Vanessa shouldered her pack with the cats tucked safely inside. She didn't bother to pack the picnic, and she carried the blanket draped over one arm. They hurried back along their tracks to the lodge, but they stopped short when the came to the parking lot.

Flames licked over the roof and smoke billowed through the windows into the sky. Fire crews and trucks surrounded the building. Dozens of people crowded behind a police cordon. Vanessa caught her breath. "The Dove's Peak Ski Lodge! It's going up in flames!"

Robert Ipswich towered over the crowd. He shook his head at the fire. "I can't believe it! I can't believe it!"

"Were you here when it started?" Vanessa asked him.

He passed his hand over his eyes. "I went into town for lunch. I just got back a few minutes ago."

"Do you know what happened?" she asked.

He waved his hand at the burning building. "Take a look. It's my office and the staff section going up in flames."

Vanessa started back. "Could it be arson?"

Robert let out a shaky breath. "I don't know what to think."

"The real question is," Pete interrupted, "Was anyone harmed?"

"No, thankfully, the fire alarm cleared everyone out. The building is empty," Robert explained. "The lodge has insurance to take care of the damages. It will also replace everything that was in your rooms."

Vanessa took the pack off her shoulders. She reached inside and patted the heads of all three cats. "I'm so happy you're safe," Vanessa murmured. Henry purred as she ran her hand along his back.

"I've arranged for you and the staff and everyone else whose rooms were damaged to stay at the Willow Brook Ski Lodge down the street.

Brandon is coming to pick you up and take you there," Robert told them.

At that moment, a big transport van pulled up to the curb with Brandon at the wheel. "All aboard!"

Robert pressed Pete's hand. "You go ahead. I'll handle things on this end. You get settled at the Willow Brook, and I'll see you later."

Pete and Vanessa climbed into the van and away they went. They found Sally at the front desk of the Willow Brook Lodge. "I'm here to handle everything for the Dove's Peak guests. If you need anything at all, just ask me. We have an open ticket from the insurance company to cover everything—and I mean *everything*."

"We've got nothing but the clothes on our backs," Vanessa told her, "and my cats."

"Don't worry about a thing." Sally handed her a key. "Here's the key to your room. Go have a hot bath and leave everything to me." She grinned at Vanessa. "I think you'll find your room a little bigger than your last one."

Vanessa glanced down at the key. "Room 401."

They took the elevator to the fourth floor and found only two doors on the landing. Pete frowned. "These better not be another one of Robert's jokes."

Vanessa unlocked the door. It opened into an enormous suite with a jacuzzi pool looking out through floor-to-ceiling windows over the snowy mountains. Vanessa set down her backpack, and the three cats sprang out. They tore under the furniture and vanished into the closets.

Vanessa opened her mouth to call them back.

Then she let her shoulders sag. "Maybe they'll be happy to stay here instead of running off all the time."

Pete gazed through the windows at the view. "This is a step up from our last room."

Vanessa sat down on one of the couches. "This is positively palatial."

A knock on the door made her get up again. She found Sally on the landing with a large shopping bag in her hand. "Here you go. It isn't much, but it will keep you going for a few days."

Vanessa's eyes widened. "What is it?"

"It's just a few changes of clothes from the Willow Brook gift shop," Sally replied. "Robert is arranging a shopping trip into town with gift vouchers from the lodge to replace everything you lost in the fire."

Vanessa gasped. "He didn't have to do that."

"It's all covered by the insurance," Sally told him.

The elevator slid open behind her, and Detective Phil Maskey emerged onto the landing. He tipped his hat to Vanessa. "They told me at the front desk I would find you here."

Pete came up behind Vanessa. "What can we do for you, Detective?"

"Tiffany Harley is missing," he replied. "I don't suppose any of you has an idea where she might be."

Vanessa and Sally exchanged glances. "No idea at all. We haven't seen her since last night."

"When was the last time you saw her?" he asked.

"She was tending bar in the dining room at the Dove's Peak Ski Lodge last night." Vanessa waved toward Sally. "Sally and her dad Frank were standing there with me."

"And none of you saw her since then?" he asked.

"I saw her take a rack of water glasses to the dish washing station," Sally replied. "That was after the guests finished dinner and the staff was cleaning up the dining room for the night."

"What time was that?" the detective asked. "Can you remember?"

Sally put her head on one side. "It must have been about nine o'clock. I went back to my room after that, and when I turned on the TV, the nine o'clock news was just ending."

Detective Phil nodded. "That's what I thought." He started to turn away.

"Do you suspect foul play in this fire?" Vanessa asked.

"Tiffany Harley had a criminal record in California," he told her. "She was wanted for armed robbery, and she fled the state to escape capture. Now it looks like she robbed the Dove's Peak Ski Lodge office. We have a warrant out for her arrest for arson and murder."

"Murder!" Vanessa cried.

"If she started that fire," Pete replied, "she could have killed Joan. Maybe Joan suspected her of robbing the lodge, or Joan could have caught her in the act. That could be why she killed Joan."

Detective Phil nodded and headed for the

elevator. "You'll let me know if you see her, won't you?"

Pete nodded. "If we see or find out anything, you'll be the first to know."

The elevator closed on Detective Phil Maskey. Sally let out her breath. "That guy makes me nervous."

Vanessa chuckled. "I think he must be slightly eccentric."

Pete turned back into the room. "That's putting it mildly."

Sally smiled. "Robert sent you an invitation to dinner with Brandon and the Dove's Peak staff. We'll see you downstairs at six o'clock sharp."

Vanessa stared at her. "Again? This is over the top."

"The insurance is taking care of everything," Sally replied. "I wouldn't be surprised if he comped your whole stay, with all your expenses paid for the rest of the weekend."

Vanessa shut the door and opened the shopping bag. She lifted out an expensive woolen sweater and a silk blouse. Her eyes popped out of her head. "This stuff is top of the line."

"They have to compensate us for the things we lost destroyed in the fire." Pete peeked into the bag. "Is there anything in there for me?"

Vanessa handed him a leather jacket, a pair of blue jeans, and a new shirt. There was also a leather belt, a pair of leather boots, and woolen socks. She found a beautiful woven shawl and a cashmere skirt at the bottom of the bag. "If this is what it means to be inconvenienced, please let me be inconvenienced more often."

Pete slipped into the leather jacket. "I've never had one of these in my life."

Vanessa took her things toward the bathroom. "I'm going to have a shower and change. It's almost dinner time."

Pete waved toward the window. "Don't you want to take advantage of the jacuzzi?"

CHAPTER 7

— ❖ —

Staff and guests from the Dove's Peak Lodge packed the Willow Brook dining room. Everyone sat around the long dining table with wide eyes. "Can you believe what they're saying about Tiffany?"

"I never would have known she was a wanted criminal."

"The police are after her. They say she killed Joan."

Frank Bendall spoke up. "What makes them think she did it? Tiffany had no more motive than anybody else."

"They have nothing to connect Tiffany to the murder," Brandon replied. "They have to suspect someone. Tiffany has a criminal record, and now she's disappeared right after a suspicious fire destroyed the office at the lodge. She's the prime suspect, but that doesn't mean she killed Joan."

"Even if Tiffany did have a criminal record and robbed the lodge," Vanessa pointed out, "she had no reason to kill Joan. If Joan caught her doing something illegal, all she had to do was run away. Killing Joan would only get her into more trouble she didn't want."

"Joan was the easiest person in the world to hate," Robert replied. "She flaunted her money everywhere she went and treated everyone she met like dirt."

Vanessa turned to Brandon. "What was it like dating her?"

Brandon's head whipped around. "How did you know about that?"

Vanessa shrugged. "A little bird told me."

Brandon laughed. "She wasn't so stuck on herself when she was young. She was wild and crazy, and I guess I was wild and crazy, too. I liked that about her. I didn't realize until I got older how dangerous she was."

"What do you mean by dangerous?" Vanessa asked.

"She got away with everything because of her father," Brandon replied. "She got arrested for shoplifting in town, and she did every drug she could get her hands on. Any time she got into trouble, her father bailed her out and greased as many palms as necessary to hush it all up."

"It wasn't just shoplifting and drugs, either," Frank chimed in. "She would have lost her license for drunk driving if her father hadn't paid off the police. He got so tired of bailing her out he sent her to school in Europe."

Brandon rounded on him. "I didn't know about that. Joan told me she was too good for the American way of life. She thought it was savage and backward."

"Savage and backward!" Vanessa repeated. "Did she use those exact words?"

"Many times," Brandon answered.

Vanessa shook her head. "How could anyone be so disdainful toward their country?"

"Joan was disdainful of everything," Robert replied. "Her country didn't mean anything more to her than the people in it."

"That's why she wanted to go to Europe," Brandon stated.

"No, it wasn't," Frank interrupted. "It was to escape her past and the law. Everyone keeps talking about Tiffany's criminal record. The police should look into Joan's for a change."

Pete and Vanessa exchanged glances. Vanessa stood up. "I better check on my cats. Thank you both again for the wonderful dinner and the clothes. This is turning out to be the best vacation I've ever had."

Pete followed her out to the lobby. He took her hand while they waited for the elevator. "The best vacation you ever had, huh? Are you sure it's the good food and the nice clothes that make it the best? Or is it the murder mystery?"

Vanessa grinned at him. "Don't tell anybody."

"I don't think I would be enjoying myself half as much without a mystery to solve, either," he murmured.

Vanessa squeezed his hand. "We are a pair, aren't we?"

"I don't know about a pair," he replied. "But I'm a cop, and I don't stop being a cop when I go on vacation."

They rode up to the fourth floor. Darkness enveloped their suite, but they didn't turn on the lights. The ghostly glow of the moon on the snowy mountains outside shone through the big windows and gave the suite a tranquil atmosphere. Pete and Vanessa stood in front of the windows, still hand in hand, and gazed out at the view.

Aurora rubbed against Vanessa's leg and mewed. "All right, darling. I'll let you out. You've been stuck in here half the day, and you can't sneak out of this room as easily as you could at the Dove's Peak staff bunk room."

She slid back the door, and the little kitten scampered onto the balcony. Henry and Flossy followed her, and the cats tiptoed along the railing. A breath of wind puffed through the door. Vanessa put her face through the opening. "It's warm outside. I think I'll go out, too."

They stepped through the sliding glass doorway onto the balcony. The moon spread its unearthly glow over the white landscape and blue sparks of light shimmered on the hills. The sound of a motor drew their attention to the parking lot.

Below them, a lone figure strode out of the lodge to the lines of black shapes set in rows in front of the building. A car hummed along the road, and its headlights glanced through the trees. The figure ventured into the parking lot and stopped next to a brown sedan.

"It's Robert," Pete murmured. "What's he doing out at this time of night?"

"He must have left the dining room right after us," Vanessa replied.

Robert jingled his keys in his hand and popped the trunk. The front passenger door opened, and another figure got out of the car. The person wore ski goggles and a full-length ski suit. The figure headed to the trunk and stood next to Robert. Robert stood a head taller than his companion. They exchanged snatches of conversation, but

Vanessa couldn't make out what they were saying.

Robert bent down and lifted a packed duffel bag out of the trunk. He slung it over his shoulder, and both figures headed into the lodge. Just before they passed under Pete and Vanessa's balcony, another car ran along the road. Its headlights touched the strange person's head, and a flash of blazing red showed clear and bright in the moonlight. Vanessa gasped. "It's Tiffany!"

Pete grabbed her hand. "Come on."

They hurried out of the room. Vanessa tapped her foot in anticipation while they waited for the elevator. They found Sally at the front desk. She smiled at them, but Vanessa didn't stop for idle talk. "Hi, Sally. Can you tell me where Robert Ipswich is staying?"

Sally's eyes widened. "He's in Room #303. It's another suit like yours, just one floor down from you."

Vanessa pressed her hand. "Thanks."

They hurried back to the elevator and rode back to the third floor. They knocked on Robert's door. He smiled when he saw them. "Well, look who's here. What are you guys doing abroad? I thought you'd be bedding down with your cats."

Pete wasn't smiling. "We're not the only ones who are here. We know you've got Tiffany in there with you."

The smile evaporated off Robert's face. "I don't know what you're talking about."

Pete waved his hand. "We just saw you two come in from the car. You should be more careful.

You know Tiffany is wanted in connection with the fire at the lodge and with Joan's death. You're implicating yourself by keeping her here with you."

Before Robert could answer, the bathroom door inside the suite opened, and Tiffany came out with a towel wrapped around her head. She stopped in her tracks when she spotted Pete and Vanessa at the door.

Pete clenched his jaw and turned away. "I'm going to have to report both of you to the police."

Robert put out his hand to stop him. "You don't have to do that."

"I'm a sworn police officer," Pete told him. "I might not be on duty here, but I have a responsibility to report this. The police want to question Tiffany about the fire, and when I tell them I found her in your room, they'll want to question you, too. You two could have conspired to kill Joan and destroy the lodge to bury the evidence."

Robert held him back. "Don't do this. We've been friends a long time. You know me well enough to know I wouldn't kill anybody. This is all a big misunderstanding."

"You were as angry as anybody that Joan was going to shut down the lodge," Pete returned. "You had a motive to kill her."

"You got it all wrong," Robert replied. "I wasn't angry about it. I just had to act that way to keep up appearances with the staff. No one knew I was working with Joan to complete the timeshare deal."

Vanessa gasped, and Pete's mouth fell open. "What?!"

Robert nodded. "We were business partners. Joan could never have completed the deal without my help. She couldn't even read the accounts. I invested all my savings in the project, and I signed the contract today for the developers to take over the lodge."

Vanessa spoke up. "But we heard the deal fell through after Joan died. The staff is relieved that the lodge is going to stay open after all."

Robert shook his head. "I don't know who told you that, but it's wishful thinking. Joan never signed the papers to complete the deal, but I'm the surviving partner. I was able to finalize the deal when the developers came to me this morning."

"If that's true," Vanessa asked, "why is Tiffany sneaking around? The police think she robbed the lodge and set the office on fire to destroy evidence."

"She had nothing to do with the fire or with Joan's death," Robert replied. "When the lodge burned down, she got scared the police would accuse her when they found out about her past record."

"They say she's wanted in San Francisco for armed robbery," Vanessa told him.

"I'm not wanted," Tiffany replied. "I served my time and turned over a new leaf. I came out here to put my past behind me."

"We've been seeing each other for the past few months," Robert went on. "When she came to me for help, I had to protect her."

Pete shook his head. "You'll both have to come with me. You have to turn yourself into the police. If you're innocent, you can explain everything to them."

Robert caught Pete by the hand. "Don't do this to us. I'm begging you as a friend to give us a chance. The police will never believe our story. They're just looking for an excuse to arrest Tiffany, and once they get her behind bars, they'll stick this murder charge on her, too. You're the only one who can help us. Please, man, do it for the sake of our friendship."

Pete frowned. "I'm sorry. I can't. You have to come with me and explain everything to the police. It's the only way."

Robert stiffened. "You've changed, man. I thought we were friends."

"You've changed, too," Pete replied. "My friend Robert would never sell out the Dove's Peak community to developers, and he would never hide a wanted fugitive in his room. I expected better from you."

He took Tiffany by the arm and led her out of the room. The party stopped at the elevator, and Pete murmured to Vanessa. "I'll see you back at our room."

Vanessa nodded, and when the elevator closed and rode downstairs, she waited on the landing for the next one going up. On the way up to the fourth floor, she turned the case over in her mind. If Tiffany didn't kill Joan or burn down the lodge, who did? Who had more motive to kill Joan to save the lodge? And who would benefit the most from the lodge staying open after Joan died?

Their conversation with Robert repeated in her mind. She got so absorbed in the case that she walked out of the elevator onto the fourth-floor landing in a dream. She almost stepped on Henry in front of her suite.

"Oh, Henry," she exclaimed. "I thought you were in the room."

Henry meowed up at her.

Vanessa stopped and stared down at him. "I was thinking the same thing. All the evidence is right here in front of us. We just need to piece it all together to catch the killer. The answer is staring us in the face if we can only see it."

Henry didn't respond. He stared at something behind her.

"What is it, Henry?" she asked. "What's on your mind?"

He set off down the hall and stopped in front of

another door.

Vanessa frowned. "Is this it? Is this the killer's room."

Henry sneezed and startled Vanessa.

"I don't understand you," she told him. "If the killer isn't in this room, what is it you're trying to show me?"

He stared up at her with his bright green eyes.

Vanessa turned around but stopped and stared at a framed photograph hung on the wall. Vanessa studied it up close. Frank Bendall stood in the midst of a crowd of cheering admirers. His face bore none of the lines of age and care he wore now, and a triumphant smile filled his face. The people on either side of him carried signs. *Calgary '88 or bust! Go Frank!* and *Hometown Hero!*

Vanessa sighed and lifted the picture off the wall. "So that's what you wanted to show me."

She gazed at the youthful hero in the photograph. "He had so much promise, and he lost it all to someone else's carelessness."

Henry blinked and turned his head away.

Vanessa glanced down at him. "You're right, Henry. I was thinking the very same thing myself. Being bitter about it doesn't give him the right to kill her."

Vanessa picked up Henry and carried both him and the photograph back to her room.

CHAPTER 8

P ete and Vanessa hopped off the chairlift and pushed their way to the top of the slopes. "Are you sticking with the beginner slope again?"

Vanessa nodded. "I'm not ready to move up to the intermediate slope yet. Maybe tomorrow."

"We're leaving tomorrow," Pete reminded her. "It's today or not at all."

"Then I'll wait until our next ski vacation," she replied. "I want to get comfortable on the beginner slope before I challenge myself. I almost broke my neck on the beginner slope yesterday, and I would have if Frank hadn't been there. I don't want to go through that again any time soon."

Pete waved his ski pole toward the other side of the hill. "I'm going this way. I'll see you at the bottom, and we'll ride up together."

Vanessa nodded, but before they could separate, she pointed toward the chairlift. "There's Frank."

Frank stood talking to a couple of tourists. "He looks like he's in the middle of a lesson."

The couple skied away down the back of the advanced slope, and Frank headed toward Pete and Vanessa. "He's not giving a lesson now."

"Something about him doesn't make sense," Vanessa told him.

"What's that?" Pete asked.

"Don't you remember last night?" Vanessa asked. "Robert told us the rumor about the timeshare deal being off was wishful thinking.

That rumor came from Frank."

"So?" Pete asked.

"So," she replied, "he must have thought the deal was off because Joan was dead. He must have wanted it to be true."

"He didn't know Robert was Joan's business partner," Pete pointed out. "That doesn't mean he killed her."

"He said something else that struck me," Vanessa went on. "He said she wanted to go to Europe to get away from the law. He said she would have lost her license for drunk driving if her father hadn't bailed her out."

"What's unusual about that?" Pete asked.

"Not even her boyfriend Brandon knew about that," Vanessa replied. "So how did Frank know?"

"Why don't you go ask him?" Pete asked.

"I don't have to go anywhere to ask him," Vanessa replied. "Here he comes."

Frank skied up to them and smiled. "Are you still on the beginner slopes?"

Vanessa turned bright red. "I don't want to move up until I'm ready."

"I was watching you just now," Frank replied. "You're ready."

"I'm glad you think so," Vanessa told him. "But I'll give it a few more runs, I think."

Frank jammed his ski poles into the snow. "Suit yourself."

"Before you go," Vanessa called out, "I was wondering...."

He stopped and turned toward her.

"I was wondering if you could tell me more about your Olympic career," she went on. "I've never met an Olympian before.

"I told you," he replied. "I never had an Olympic career. I had hopes that were dashed by a reckless driver."

"A drunk driver?" Vanessa asked.

"That's right," Frank replied.

"Who was the driver?" Vanessa asked. "Can you tell me what happened?"

"It doesn't matter," Frank replied. "It was a long time ago. I'd just as soon forget about it."

"It does matter," Vanessa countered. "And it seems to me you've never forgotten it. It probably haunts you to this day."

He shrugged. "Maybe it does."

"Who was the drunk driver that ended your career?" Vanessa asked. "I'd like to know."

Frank rounded on her with his teeth bared. "It was Joan Pritchett, all right? Are you happy now? There, I told you. It was Joan Pritchett. Now can we stop talking about it?"

"I'm sorry to bring up such a painful memory," Vanessa replied. "I'm sure you must have been angry with her for ruining your chance to go to the Olympics."

He turned away. "I can get over it."

"But you never have," Vanessa replied.

"What difference does it make?" he snapped.

"How did you know Joan never signed the papers completing the timeshare deal?" she asked.

His head whipped around. "What did you say?"

"How did you know Joan didn't sign the papers to sell the lodge to timeshare developers?" Vanessa asked. "Everyone was relieved to hear that the lodge was staying open, but no one was as relieved as you and Sally. It turns out that rumor was not true, and the rumor came from you. How did you find that out? Did you hear it from someone else, or did you just hope it was true?"

Frank glared at her. "I don't know where I heard it."

Pete interrupted. "Where were you the night Joan was killed? Where did you go after you left the staff party?"

"I went upstairs to my room," Frank growled. "That's all you need to know."

"But your room isn't upstairs," Vanessa countered. "You stayed in the detached cabins behind the lodge. What were you doing upstairs?"

"Did you confront Joan in her room the night she was killed?" Pete asked. "Did you kill Joan to ruin the deal with the developers?"

Frank ground his teeth together, but before they could stop him, he shot forward on his skis and sailed into the air. He launched himself over the cornice onto the advanced slope and disappeared down the mountain. Pete flailed the air with his ski poles. "Quick! After him!"

In a flash, he rocketed to the edge of the slope. He hit the icy edge and took to the air. He landed on slick snow and sailed down the mountain after Frank. Vanessa stared at them with her heart in her throat. She couldn't go down there, but she couldn't let Pete down. He might need her to help catch Frank.

She took a deep breath and pushed herself over the edge. Her heart fell into her boots as the slope fell away in front of her. She looked down at empty air under her skis. She didn't even have time to scream or call for help. She tumbled headlong down the mountain. Her skis popped off and flew in all directions. She managed to let go of her ski poles before the snow tore them from her hands, too.

She cartwheeled down the slope with her eyes, nose, and mouth full of snow until she rolled to a stop. When she got her eyes open, she heard voices from somewhere above her. She shielded her eyes from the glare of the sun off the snow. Several people looked down at her from the chairlift floating over her head. They pointed at her, and some of them laughed.

Vanessa shook the snow off herself, but she couldn't help but laugh, too. She struggled to her feet. At least she didn't have her skis on. She plowed her way back up the slope to the top of the chairlift.

The other skiers watched her from the top. They snickered and whispered to each other, but Vanessa paid them no attention. She brushed the snow off her hair and jacket and shouldered her way to the chairlift operator's booth.

The operator did his best not to laugh when she explained the situation to him, and he agreed to let her ride down the mountain. She had no skis. It was either ride or walk down. He came out of his booth, caught hold of a chair, and held it for her while she got into it. Then she sailed away.

More people pointed and laughed at her riding down. Her cheeks burned, but she managed to smile and wave to them. Then she kept her eyes open for Pete. She caught sight of him near the bottom where two advanced runs met up with the beginner run near the lodge. He bent his head low and swept down the slope so fast the wind whistled in his hair.

Another figure crouched low over his skis farther ahead, and Vanessa recognized Frank. He showed no signs of stopping at the chairlift. He rocketed past the lift and around the lodge, headed for the woods on the other side. A line of wooden barricades labeled *Danger: Unmarked Area* blocked his path. He gripped his ski poles tighter and swerved around them.

Vanessa waved her arms to catch the chairlift attendant's attention. "Stop that man! Don't let him get away."

Three attendants stood around the lift. Two didn't even hear her. The third scrunched up his nose and put his hand to his ear. "Huh?"

No amount of yelling could get her message across in time. They didn't notice Frank sailing past them or Pete hot on his trail. Vanessa sank back in her seat. She couldn't do anything from up in the chairlift. She could only watch Frank ski off into the sunset. Once he entered those woods, the police would never catch him. There wasn't a single person on that mountain that could ski as fast as Frank Bendall.

At that moment, a black and white streak shot out from behind the lodge's observation deck. Frank kept his eyes on his escape route. He didn't notice the streak any more than the chairlift attendants noticed him. Nothing mattered to him as much as getting away.

Vanessa shot forward in her seat, and her breath stuck in her throat. The black streak bounded over the deck rail and across a snowdrift. Vanessa couldn't yell. She couldn't do anything more than whisper. "Flossy."

Flossy was moving too fast to stop, and she didn't see Frank, either. The freedom of the wide open ski field thrilled her to exuberant heights. She pranced and frisked like a kitten. Her black and white coat gave her perfect camouflage against the snow. Frank barreled down the slope and across the snow bank just as Flossy ran in front of his skis.

At the last second, Frank and Flossy spotted each other. Flossy froze, but Frank didn't have time to stop. Their eyes were locked in a fateful moment of destiny. Frank hit the snow bank at top speed, and his skis hissed on either side of Flossy's crouched body. The air rushing past him brushed her soft fur.

Frank stared down at the cat between his skis and tried to do something. He couldn't decide whether to brake to a stop or keep on going. He picked up one ski, and the other pivoted under him. Before he could correct himself, the one ski still on the ground skidded to one side. Frank wobbled, trying his best to keep his balance.

As Frank skied by, Flossy scampered back

toward the deck and jumped onto the railing. From there, she watched in safety as Frank catapulted past her. He attempted to put his weight on his other ski, but the damage was done. He lost his balance and crashed head first into the snow bank.

CHAPTER 9

Pete skidded to a stop next to the snow bank and stuck his poles into the snow. "Well, well. All's well that ends well."

Vanessa stumped over to the deck on her ski boots. "Good job. You caught the killer."

Pete pressed the lever to release his boots from his skis. He dug Frank out of the snow bank and hauled him to his feet. "It wasn't me. It was your cats again."

Vanessa chuckled and picked up Flossy. "How did you get out of the room, this time, Flossy? I thought I locked the door."

Frank spat snow out of his mouth and tried to shake it out of his eyes as Pete snapped his handcuffs around Frank's wrists. "Seeing Joan walking around, free as a bird after what she did to me, was living torture."

"So that's why you killed her?" Vanessa asked. "You killed her to get revenge for ruining your Olympic hopes?"

"I did no such thing!" Frank shot back. "I never had any intention of killing her. If I wanted to kill her out of revenge, I would have done it years ago. I've lived with what she did all these years and never gotten revenge."

"Then how did you wind up in her room?" Pete asked. "That was no accident."

"I went to her room to confront her about the timeshare deal," Frank replied. "This timeshare contract would have cost Sally her job. I couldn't stand by and watch Joan ruin Sally's life the way she ruined mine."

"But she wouldn't listen?" Vanessa asked.

"She never listened to anybody," Frank snapped. "It was her way or the highway. That's all you ever needed to know about Joan Pritchett."

"So what happened?" Vanessa asked.

"I started to explain that I could let the past go," Frank replied. "I could forget all the things she did to me, and I could even forget how her family ruined this town by selling out to developers. Then she got a weird look on her face and said she didn't know what I was talking about."

Vanessa and Pete frowned at each other. "What do you mean?"

Frank tried to move his arms. "Don't you see?

She had no idea who I was. She had no memory of crashing into me and wrecking my chance at the Olympics. She was out of her mind drunk. She never knew what she'd done to me, and her father hushed the whole incident up so she could leave the country."

Vanessa nodded. "So that's why you killed her."

Frank hunched his head down between his shoulders. "Killing was too good for her."

"What about the fire?" Pete asked.

Frank looked away. "I came back to the lodge early yesterday. One of my lessons was cancelled, and I had nothing else to do. I passed Robert's office and spotted him in there with the developers. I stopped by the door and overheard their conversation. I realized they were going through with the timeshare deal anyway, even though Joan was dead."

"And you thought the deal died with her, didn't you?" Vanessa asked. "That must have made you upset."

"He sold us out," Frank fumed. "Robert lied to our faces when he pretended to be mad about the timeshare deal when he was selling us out behind our backs the whole time. He was Joan's business partner, and he completed the deal after she died."

"So you started the fire," Vanessa prompted him.

Frank nodded. "I lost control. You can't imagine. What could I do? The deal was done. The lodge was sold to the developers. Sally, and I, and all the others who made this place a success—we were all out on our tails to make a buck for them. I couldn't see straight. The only thing I could think about was stopping them. So I lit the fire. I lit it behind the office to destroy any paperwork I could. It was the only thing I could do. I had to do it."

Vanessa sighed and stroked Flossy. "You didn't have to, but you did."

Pete took hold of Frank's arm. "And now you're under arrest for the murder of Joan Pritchett, and also, for the arson at Dove's Peak Ski Lodge. You have the right to remain silent....."

Vanessa listened until Pete finished reading Frank his rights, but Frank scowled in the other direction. Detective Phil arrived and took Frank into custody. He eyed Pete with a wry grin. "I don't know anybody else who goes skiing with handcuffs in their pocket."

Pete turned red. "I'm a cop."

"I'm a cop, too," Detective Phil replied. "Half the Dove's Peak police force skis on their off time, but they don't carry their handcuffs with them."

Pete shrugged. "There was a killer on the loose. I thought it might be a good idea—just this once."

Detective Phil frowned. "How did you say you caught up with him? Frank can out-ski anybody in this town."

"I knew it as soon as I saw him take that slope, there was no chance I was going to catch up with him," Pete replied. "He would have left me in the dust, but this cat ran out from behind the building and ran into his path. It distracted him, and he crashed."

Detective Phil studied Flossy nestled in

Vanessa's arms. "What's a cat doing at a ski resort?"

"She's my cat," Vanessa told him. "I left her in my room, but I guess she got out somehow."

Detective Phil shook his head. "I don't understand it, but then again, I don't understand most things in this job. As long as the suspect is in custody and has confessed to the crime, that's all I care about."

"I'm sure he'll tell you the same thing he told me," Pete replied. "And all the records of the drunk driving wreck that destroyed his career will be on file with the police department. Instead of investigating Tiffany Harley, you should take a look at Joan Pritchett's file."

Detective Phil nodded and turned away. "Funny we didn't pick up on that while we were looking into Joan's death."

"Her father used his money and influence to cover it up," Vanessa told him. "He made sure no one knew what Joan had done, and then he sent her out of the country."

"He did a lot of that," Detective Phil replied. "He used his money and influence to ruin this town along with the lives of everybody in it—and he did it all in the name of more money and influence."

Vanessa studied him. "Were you here in the days of old Mr. Pritchett."

"I was born and raised in this town," Detective Phil replied. "I've watched the whole thing from beginning to end. I can almost forgive poor old Frank for killing Joan. Half the town feels the same way he does."

"What will happen to him now?" Vanessa asked.

"Him? Oh, he's finished, all right," Detective Phil replied. "There's nothing anybody can do for him. And it looks like the Dove's Peak Ski Lodge is finished, too. That fire destroyed enough of it that it can't be brought back."

"What will happen to the timeshare deal, then?" Vanessa asked.

Detective Phil turned away. "It's dead in the water. There won't be any timeshare and good riddance."

He walked away to the parking lot, where Frank sat in the back seat of a squad car. Pete and Vanessa watched the police drive away with him. "That's it, then. The end of an era."

"So Frank succeeded," Vanessa remarked. "He

destroyed the timeshare deal, and he got rid of Joan."

"I don't think he intended it to work out this way," Pete replied.

Vanessa shook her head. "It seems a terrible shame."

Pete picked up his skis and poles. "Murder always is."

Vanessa started toward the door. "I guess I'll see you later."

He frowned. "Aren't you coming skiing again?"

"I can't," she told him. "I don't have any skis or poles."

"What happened to yours?" he asked.

She pointed up toward the advanced slope.

"They're up there. They....they fell off."

He looked right and then left. "I guess you'll have to go back to the rental shop to get another pair."

Vanessa smiled and shook her head. "For half a day's skiing? I don't think so. I think I'll just relax in our jacuzzi with a glass of wine."

"Giving up so easy?" he asked her. "Get another pair and come out with me. We were just starting to enjoy ourselves."

She smiled and shook her head again. "It's a sign that my time skiing is over—for now."

CHAPTER 10

❖

Pete and Vanessa entered the dining room of Willow Brook Ski Lodge for the last time and found the buffet tables set for lunch. The staff was all at work. Only Robert and Brandon met them at the door. Robert shook Pete's hand. "I should have known you would catch the killer. You never went off duty in your life, did you?"

Pete smiled. "I can't remember a time, now that you mention it."

"I'm sorry I doubted you," Robert told him. "I was angry when you took Tiffany in for questioning, but it was the right thing to do. The police released her without charge when you caught Frank. I should have known you would stick to the case until you found the truth. You have enough integrity for the whole police department."

"I wasn't alone in catching him." He squeezed Vanessa's hand. "I had help."

Robert shook hands with Vanessa, too. "You had a wonderful holiday here, I trust. At least you learned to ski, so the trip wasn't a complete failure, even with all the arson and murder and mayhem."

Vanessa pressed his hand. "It would have been a pretty dull holiday. I couldn't have planned a better vacation, and I'm glad I got the chance to learn to ski from the best before Frank got arrested for arson and murder."

"Everyone in town is devastated about Frank," Brandon added. "He was a staple of this community from his boyhood, and a lot of people came here to learn to ski from him. I don't know what we'll do without him."

"What about Sally?" Vanessa asked. "She might not be the Olympian her father was, but she's a very capable skier, and she loves helping people."

Brandon stroked his chin. "I didn't think of her, but you're right. She would be perfect to take her father's place. I wonder if she wants to try her hand at giving lessons."

"Frank's biggest fear was that the timeshare deal would throw Sally out in the cold without a job," Vanessa went on. "If you gave her a position as a ski instructor, you would be doing them both a big service. I'm sure the guests would appreciate her as much as they appreciated Frank."

"I was hoping to keep her on here as assistant

manager," Brandon replied. "She was the best Concierge in town at the Dove's Peak lodge. She would be taking a step down in pay to give lessons on the slopes."

Vanessa's eyes widened. "I didn't know you planned to keep her on."

Sally approached them at that moment. "I hope you weren't planning to leave without saying good-bye."

Vanessa gave her a hug. "We were just talking about your position here at the lodge, now that your father isn't giving lessons anymore."

"Brandon offered me the job of assistant manager," Sally told her.

"And I offered her a big pay raise, too," Brandon added. "She's got an apartment of her own here at the lodge. No more staff quarters for her."

"Will you take it?" Vanessa asked. "You have such a natural talent for helping people."

Sally broke into a radiant smile. "I already accepted it."

Vanessa threw her arms around Sally's neck. "Congratulations!"

"What about you?" Sally asked. "Have you got your cats all loaded up for the trip home?"

"I couldn't run the risk of them running off again," Vanessa replied. "Otherwise, I would have brought Henry to give you a good-bye kiss."

"You'll have to give him a kiss for me." Sally gazed into the distance with a wistful look on her face. "They're such wonderful cats, and so intelligent. I sometimes get the feeling Henry can understand exactly what I'm saying when I talk to him. It's like talking to an old friend."

Vanessa smiled. "I understand exactly what you mean."

"You can trust them," Sally went on. "You can share your darkest secrets, and they'll help you find the answers to your problems. It sounds crazy to say something like that about an animal, but that's the way I feel."

"It's not crazy at all," Vanessa told her. "I confide in my cats all the time, and I can't tell you how many problems they've helped me solve. I meant what I said about finding a cat for you. Now that you've got your own apartment, you could keep a cat for a pet. Are you still interested?"

"Could you find me a cat like Henry?" Sally asked. "Could you find me a cat that understands me when I talk to him?"

Vanessa smiled. "I'm certain of it."

Sally clasped her hands. "That would be wonderful. Do you have a cat in particular in mind for me?"

"I would recommend adopting Aurora," Vanessa replied. "She's still a kitten, but I think she's too attached to my other cats now. I'll have to find you a very special cat of your own."

Sally hugged her again. "I can't wait! I would love a cat of my own. I would do everything for them, and I would make sure they had the best of everything."

"That's settled then." Vanessa looked around. "I hope you weren't planning on leaving before lunch."

Pete laughed. "With a spread like this waiting for us? Never!"

Robert flagged down a waitress and raised a glass. "Here's to you two. Make sure it's not another five years before I see you again."

Pete touched his glass to Robert's. "No. I promise."

They sat down and ate a hearty lunch until Pete pushed back his chair and put down his napkin. "It's time we headed home, or we'll be spending another night here."

Hugs and well wishes flowed all around. Robert and Brandon couldn't stop shaking Pete's hand all the way out to the parking lot, and Sally couldn't stop embracing Vanessa.

The freezing cold wind and fluttering snow

in the parking lot drove the locals back to the shelter of the lodge's entrance. Pete and Vanessa tore themselves away and, with a last wave, they hurried to their car. The cats lounged in their new carriers on the back seat.

Vanessa slammed her door and huddled into her coat. "Let's get out of here."

Pete fired up the engine. "Be it ever so humble, there's no place like home."

He eased out of the parking lot. He turned on the heater and the windshield wipers. "That was quite the send off."

"That's because we caught the killer for them," Vanessa replied.

"We didn't catch him," Pete countered. "Flossy did."

"We work as a team," Vanessa replied. "And Henry gave me the final clue to the mystery."

"The cats will be happy to get back to the Sanctuary where they can run around," Pete went on. "I understand why they didn't like being cooped up in the room all the time."

"I should be grateful they got out the way they did," Vanessa replied. "We would never have solved the mystery if they hadn't."

"We might have solved the mystery," Pete told her, "but we would never have caught Frank if Flossy hadn't run out in front of him the way she did. I wish I had a video camera for that."

Vanessa laughed. "You say that every time one of my cats catches a murderer. I wish I had a dollar for every time you've said that."

"If I had a video recording of every daring arrest your cats have made," Pete countered, "I would be a millionaire."

"And my cats would be trotted out in front of the world television audience to show their skills," Vanessa pointed out. "And none of us would have our peaceful life at the Sanctuary."

Pete shot her a sidelong grin. "Whoever told you your life was peaceful?"

Vanessa squeezed his hand. "Okay, so it's not very peaceful."

The windshield wipers beat back and forth in time, and the snow built up on the edges of the windshield. Even with the heater on, Vanessa shivered. "I hope Sam's getting along all right."

"I'm sure he's just fine," Pete replied. "We could keep driving if you want to. We don't ever have to go back."

"And leave your precious homicide squad without its fearless leader?" Vanessa teased. "You know you wouldn't be happy with that."

"You're right." He switched on the headlights. "I guess we better go back."

"We can always take another vacation," she told him. If we didn't go home, it's not really a vacation, is it?"

"Next time we go on vacation," Pete told her, "let's go somewhere warm."

"How about the Bahamas?" Vanessa suggested. "I've always wanted to go there."

Pete's eyes lit up, and he grinned at her. "Hey, I could teach you to snorkel."

The End

Thank you for purchasing, downloading and reading my book. I strive to create stories that my readers will love. If you enjoyed this book I would be very grateful if you posted a short review.

Thank you for purchasing this book and thank you for your support.

For other books by Nancy C. Davis Visit:

Catcozymysteries.com

Your Free Gifts

Visit the Following link to Receive 3 Free
Mini Cozy Mysteries

http://catcozymysteries.com/masp

Made in the USA
Lexington, KY
01 May 2016